For Elsie Grace Colley,
thank you for being Unicorn's biggest fan –
she thinks you're amazing too! – EA

For Eva, my biggest fan x – KH

Published in the UK by Scholastic, 2021
Euston House, 24 Eversholt Street, London, NW1 1DB
Scholastic Ireland, 89E Lagan Road, Dublin Industrial Estate, Glasnevin, Dublin, D11 HP5F

SCHOLASTIC and associated logos are trademarks and/or
registered trademarks of Scholastic Inc.

Text © Emma Adams, 2021
Illustrations © Katy Halford, 2021

The rights of Emma Adams and Katy Halford to be identified
as the author and illustrator of this work have been asserted
by them under the Copyright, Designs and Patents Act 1988.

PB ISBN 978 0 702305 56 6
HB ISBN 978 0 702311 95 6

A CIP catalogue record for this book is available from the British Library.

Printed in China
Paper made from wood grown in sustainable forests and other controlled sources.

1 3 5 7 9 10 8 6 4 2

www.scholastic.co.uk

Unicorn and the Rainbow Poop Save Christmas

Emma Adams and Katy Halford

SCHOLASTIC

It's wintertime in Happyville,
there's magic in the air.
A party's happening nearby,
I wonder who is there . . .

There's Unicorn!
And **Witch** – oh look,
there's **Dragon** sipping tea.

And Mr Knight is snuggled up,
he's snoring quietly.

The **elves** are shaking **glitter**
as they decorate the tree,

while **Wizard** sings songs loudly
and then dances merrily.

LA

LA

LA

BAUBLES

GLITTER

What are they up to? you might ask.
What can all this be for?
The arts and crafts, the paper chains
(the mess that's on the floor).

They're getting ready for some fun – it's just that time of year,
because, you may have guessed it, yes . . . **Christmas** is almost here!

But suddenly —

"Knock,
knock!" said Elf,
"a letter's here for you."

A letter? How exciting!
Unicorn let out a
"Wooo!"

Who was it from? What was it for?
"Please read!" everyone cried.

But as she started reading,
Unicorn went quite wide-eyed . . .

Dear Unicorn, it said in very big and swirly writing,

I have a favour I must ask, - it really is exciting.
You see, I've got a tummy ache, it's awful and it hurts.
I can't eat all my favourite foods - not even nice desserts.

So . . . can you do my job for me? It comes with lots of perks.
The sleigh, the presents, cookies too-you're welcome to the works.

Of course, you could say no but then this is <u>such</u> a good cause,
so . . . let me know ASAP.

Sincerely,
Santa Claus

THE NORTH POLE

SANTA'S WORKSHOP
NORTH POLE
ELF APPROVED

"Oh no, Santa is poorly!" cried the elves in pure dismay.
"It's **our** job to save Christmas – to the North Pole! Right away!"

They packed their bags and warmest coats
– they left an awful mess.

But super-fast they jumped aboard . . .

... the North-bound
Claus Express!

The train was so **magnificent**
in red, gold, white and green.

Choo! Choo!

For certain the **best** train that they had **ever** seen.

It chug-chug-chugged on icy tracks,

it whizzed throughout the night.

Past shining lakes and tall fir trees,

towards a distant light.

LITTLE RED WAS HERE

GRIMM'S PIT STOP

NORTH POLE

HAPPYVILLE

Then, "There it is!" cried someone from their cabin in First Class –
they tried to get a better look but just steamed up the glass.

And as the train arrived and all the wheels slowed to a roll,
a smiling lady said, "Welcome, dear friends, to the North Pole!"

The lady (well, that's Mrs Claus), she told them all about
how Santa Claus was so poorly that he could not go out.

"There is one other thing," she said,
"that we forgot to say –
the reindeer are quite ill as well,
so they can't pull the sleigh."

No Santa and no reindeer,
oh my goodness, what a mess!

How could they all save Christmas now?
There's just no way. Unless . . .

"Prepare the sleigh!" called Unicorn,
"I think I've got a plan."

She gave a whinny,
    stamped her hooves
        and quickly off she ran.

The elves were waiting patiently – they'd crowded in the hall,
and pushed the big doors open as the snow began to fall.
They heard the ting-a-ling of bells, and suddenly a

"Neigh!"

"It's Unicorn!" everyone cheered.
"She's pulling Santa's sleigh!"

Soon Unicorn began to run, she sped past all the crowds,
then through the doors, into the snow and . . .

... Up into the clouds!

That night they flew around the world as everybody slept.

From child to child in every land,
across the sky they swept.

The **elves** were super speedy –
so much faster than the rest.

And **Wizard**? Well, he tried his best
but often got quite stressed.

The **witches** used their magic
and the **dragons** helped out too,

while Princess ate the cookies
(though, she also shared a few).

Then, just at the last moment, Unicorn would quietly snoop . . .

. . . to leave an extra present
– yes, a sparkly

rainbow

poop!

You see, our dear friend Unicorn
knows how to save the day . . .

...a **sparkly** rainbow Christmas full of **fun**

— hip, hip, hooray!